Flo & Wendell
EXPLORE

William Wegman

Dial Books for Young Readers
An imprint of Penguin Group (USA) LLC

for Atlas & Lola

DIAL BOOKS FOR YOUNG READERS
Published by the Penguin Group • Penguin Group (USA) LLC
375 Hudson Street, New York, New York 10014

USA / Canada / UK / Ireland / Australia / New Zealand / India / South Africa / China
penguin.com • A Penguin Random House Company

Text copyright © 2014 by William Wegman
Pictures copyright © 2014 by William Wegman

Library of Congress Cataloging-in-Publication Data • Wegman, William. • Flo & Wendell explore / by William Wegman. • pages cm • Summary: When Flo takes her little brother, Wendell, camping in their backyard, they use their imaginations to have the best adventure ever. • ISBN 978-0-8037-3930-7 (hardcover) • [1. Camping—Fiction. 2. Brothers and sisters—Fiction. 3. Weimaraner (Dog breed)—Fiction. 4. Dogs—Fiction.] I. Title. II. Title: Flo and Wendell explore. • PZ7.W4234Flr 2014 • [E]—dc23 • 2014001606

Designed by Jason Burch and Emily Helck • Text set in Fiesole. • Manufactured in China on acid-free paper
10 9 8 7 6 5 4 3 2 1

The artwork for this book was created with gouache on photographs.

With special thanks to: Jason Burch, Emily Helck and Christine Burgin, Jake Wotherspoon, Gene and Renée LaFollette, Brian and Beth Meany, Nancy Conescu and Lily Malcom, Ken Swezey, Dorian Karchmar.

Every year, Flo and her little brother, Wendell,
go on vacation with their parents.

This year, they went on a camping trip
in their uncle Mervin's big RV.

Flo had a lovely time.

But Wendell? Not so much. All they did was drive around, drive around, drive around!

He didn't once get to use his souvenir hatchet.

So Flo promised to take Wendell on a *real* camping adventure. They would sleep in a real tent. Wendell would get to do everything he wanted to do.

What to bring, what to bring, what to bring?

Flo led the way.

In no time, they found the perfect place to pitch their tent.

It was more difficult
than they imagined.

All those flaps
and poles and
stakes!

What next? Fishing!

They let all the fish go. All except for one small
tuna from a can, which they ate for lunch.

Now, where could they find a canoe?

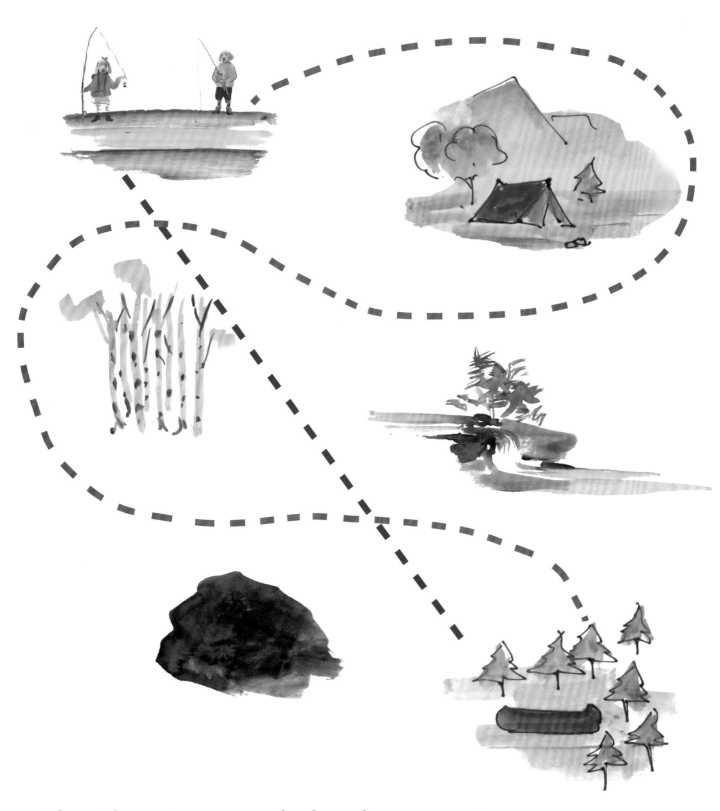

Aha! There it was, tucked under some pines.

The canoe was heavy, but together
they made light of it.

Flo was an expert. She must have picked up her technique from one of those nature shows.

Up ahead . . . Rapids!

They might need a little more practice.

Just then they saw something scary. What was it? A bear!

Flo and Wendell were very still.

So was the bear.

Actually it didn't move at all.

Phew!

A ROCK

This time Wendell took the lead.

He knew a shortcut.

Good thing he
had his hatchet.

Suddenly everything looked familiar.

It was their campsite! Exactly how they left it.
There was just one more thing to do . . .

Toast marshmallows! Flo liked hers lightly browned and Wendell liked his incinerated.

Finally Wendell was happy,
and Flo was too.